The Hockey Card

Story by **Jack Siemiatycki** and **Avi Slodovnick**

Illustrated by **Doris Barrette**

Lobster Press ™

Siemiatycki, Jack, 1946-
Slodovnick, Avi, 1962-
The Hockey Card
Text © 2002 Jack Siemiatycki & Avi Slodovnick
Illustrations © 2002 Doris Barrette

Published by Lobster Press™
1620 Sherbrooke Street West, Suites C & D, Montréal, Québec   H3H 1C9
Tel. (514) 904-1100 • Fax (514) 904-1101 • www.lobsterpress.com

Publisher: Alison Fripp
To my mother, with love and thanks

Editor: Jane Pavanel

Design & layout: Marielle Maheu

Distributed in the United States by: Distributed in Canada by:
Publishers Group West   Raincoast Books
1700 Fourth Street   9050 Shaughnessey Street
Berkeley, CA 94710   Vancouver, BC V6P 6E5

We acknowledge the financial support of the Government of Canada through the Book Publishing Industry Development Program (BPIDP) for our publishing activities.

The Canada Council | Le Conseil des Arts
for the Arts | du Canada

We acknowledge the support of the Canada Council for the Arts for our publishing program.

SODEC
SOCIÉTÉ DE DÉVELOPPEMENT
DES ENTREPRISES CULTURELLES
Québec ▪▪

National Library of Canada Cataloguing in Publication

Slodovnick, Avi, 1962-

    The Hockey Card / Avi Slodovnick, Jack Siemiatycki ; Doris Barrette, illustrator.

ISBN 1-894222-65-2

    1. Hockey—Juvenile fiction. I. Barrette, Doris II. Siemiatycki, Jack III. Title.

PS8587.L63H62 2002   jC813'.6   C2002-901400-X
PZ7

Printed in Hong Kong, China

To Emma, Kate, Paul, Noam, Mark and Debbie, all of them, like us, lifelong hockey fans.
- Jack and Avi

To my brothers, Mario, François, André, Benoît, Christian, Yvon and Ugo.
- Doris Barrette

Last Saturday was my birthday and my Uncle Jack came over to watch the hockey game with me and my dad. At the end of the first period, Uncle Jack announced that he'd found his old hockey cards. He and my dad were really excited.

When it was time for bed, Uncle Jack came
to tuck me in. "I have a story to tell you," he said.
"It's about the best hockey card I ever had."

When Uncle Jack was a kid, all the boys at his
school collected hockey cards. They traded them
too, and played flipping and tossing games like "odds
or evens" and "closest to the wall." They played to try
to win cards from each other. Every boy wanted to
have the most cards.

In class, the minutes dragged until recess. As soon as the bell rang, everyone rushed into the hallway and down the stairs. They couldn't wait to get outside.

One day, Sylvester Kornpot challenged Uncle Jack
to a game of odds or evens, winner take all. Sylvester
was the biggest hockey card shark in the whole school.

Everyone was afraid to play him, even Uncle Jack. But he knew if he refused, the boys would call him "chicken." Uncle Jack agreed to meet Sylvester at lunchtime. They would play until one of them had won all of the other one's cards.

When the lunch bell rang, Uncle Jack walked on shaky legs to the schoolyard. Sylvester looked him in the eye and said, "I'm odds, you're evens."

Facing each other, they began to play. At first, it seemed like the match could go either way — Sylvester won some of Uncle Jack's cards, then Uncle Jack won some of Sylvester's cards. But as the crowd around them grew, there was a shift in the game. Sylvester began winning more and more of Uncle Jack's cards.

Uncle Jack had a terrible feeling in the pit of his stomach. He was down to his last two cards and there was no way he could win the other ones back. To make matters worse, some of the boys were laughing at him.

One kid even shouted, "Sucker!"

Uncle Jack flipped and lost. That left him with only one card. But it wasn't just any card. It was his favorite. It was a card of Maurice "the Rocket" Richard, the greatest hockey player who ever lived.

Uncle Jack felt like crying. If he lost, he would never see his Rocket Richard card again. But he had agreed to play winner take all. Pretending to scratch his forehead, he lifted the card to his lips and kissed it quickly, hoping no one would see.

Uncle Jack held his breath and let the card go. As it flipped through the air, he closed his eyes. He couldn't bear to watch. The crowd was silent.

He looked at the ground. Lying face-up was Maurice Richard. Also face-up was a player from the Toronto Maple Leafs. Uncle Jack had won the round!

Now he had to decide which of the two cards to flip next. He was afraid to lose the Rocket, but at the same time he wasn't afraid. As he picked up the cards, he glanced at the picture of his favorite player. He could have sworn Rocket Richard winked at him.

He decided to flip the Rocket Richard card. It won!
Again and again, Uncle Jack went with the Rocket.
Each time, the cards turned up evens. One by one,
Uncle Jack and the Rocket were winning Sylvester's
cards. Sylvester looked miserable.

By now the crowd was cheering. Nothing like this had ever happened before. Sylvester Kornpot had only one card left. They flipped and Uncle Jack won! The game was over. The Rocket was unbeatable.

W hen Uncle Jack finished telling me the story, I asked him if it was true. He reached into his pocket and pulled out a hockey card. It was bent at the corners and the colors were faded.

"This is for you," he said with a smile. "Happy birthday."

It was Uncle Jack's Maurice "the Rocket" Richard card.

I flipped the card just like my Uncle Jack did when he was a boy, and when I looked down, I could have sworn Maurice Richard winked at me.